THE USE OF PHOTOGRAPHY

ANNIE ERNAUX
MARC MARIE

TRANSLATED BY
ALISON L. STRAYER

THE USE OF PHOTOGRAPHY

SEVEN STORIES PRESS
New York * Oakland * London

Originally published in French as
L'usage de la photo (Paris: Gallimard, 2005).

Photos courtesy of the authors.

SEVEN STORIES PRESS
140 Watts Street
New York, NY 10013
www.sevenstories.com

LIBRARY OF CONGRESS CATALOGING-IN-PUBLICATION DATA
is on file.

College professors and high school and middle school teachers may order free examination copies of Seven Stories Press titles. Visit https://www.sevenstories.com/pg/resources-academics or email academic@sevenstories.com.

PRINTED IN
United States of America

9 8 7 6 5 4 3 2 1

“Eroticism is the approval of life unto death.”

—GEORGES BATAILLE

Often, from the start of our relationship, on getting up in the morning, I would gaze in fascination at the dinner table, which had not been cleared, at the chairs out of place, our tangled clothes that had been thrown all over the floor the night before, while we were making love. It was a different landscape every time. Having to destroy it by separating and picking up each of our belongings made my heart heavy. I felt as if I were removing the only objective trace of our pleasure.

One morning, I got up after M. had left. When I came downstairs and saw the pieces of clothing and lingerie, the shoes, scattered over the tiles of the corridor in the sunlight, I had a sensation of sorrow and beauty. For the first time, I thought that this arrangement born of desire and accident, doomed to disappear, should be photographed. I went to get my camera. When I told M. what I had done, he confessed to having felt the same desire.

Tacitly, from that time on, as if making love were not enough and we needed to preserve a material representation of the act, we continued to take photos. Some we took immediately after lovemaking, others the next morning. The morning pictures were the most moving. These things cast off by our bodies had spent the whole night in the very place and position in which they'd fallen, the remains of an already distant celebration. To see them again in the light of day was to feel the passage of time.

Very soon we grew eager, even excited to discover together and to photograph the always new and unpredictable composition, whose elements—sweaters, stockings, shoes—had organized themselves according to unknown laws, movements and gestures that we had forgotten, of which we had been unaware.

A rule was spontaneously established between us: never to touch the arrangement of the clothing. To move a high-heeled shoe or a T-shirt would have been wrong, as impossible for me as changing the order of the words in my journal. It would have been an attack on the reality of our act of love. And if one of us had, without thinking, picked up a piece of clothing, it was not put back for the photograph.

M. usually took several shots of the scene, framing them differently to capture all the things scattered on the floor. I preferred him to do the shooting. Unlike him, I have little experience of photography, which I've only practiced in a sporadic, absent-minded way until now. At first he used the heavy black Samsung that belonged to me, then the Minolta that had belonged to his late father, and later the small Olympus that replaced my faulty Samsung. All three were analog cameras.[1]

There was a delay of one or several weeks (the time it took to finish the film and bring it to Photo Service for development) between our taking the photos and viewing them for the first time, which was done according to a ritual:

* the person who went to collect the prints was not allowed to open the packet;
* both of us had to be sitting on the sofa, side by side, with a drink in front of us and a CD playing in the background; and
* the photos were to be removed from the envelope one at a time and viewed by both of us.

Each time was a surprise. We did not immediately recognize the room in the house where the photo had been taken, or the clothing. It was no longer the scene we had seen and wanted to save, soon to be lost, but a strange painting, with often sumptuous colors and enigmatic shapes. We felt as if the lovemaking of the night or the morning, the date of which we already struggled to recall, had taken on material form and at the same time been transfigured, as if it now existed *elsewhere*, in a mysterious space.

For a few months, it was enough for us to simply take photos, to view and to accumulate them. The idea of writing

---

1 This term, which has appeared in recent years to mark the difference from "digital," just as vinyl marks the difference from CD in music, is a distinction that heralds the programmed disappearance of the former in favor of the latter. It strikes me as incongruous, impossible to apply to what for me will remain forever, simply, *a camera*.

about them came up one evening over dinner. I don't remember who had the idea first, but we knew at once that we shared the same desire to give it substance. It was as if what we'd thought until then would be enough to preserve a trace of our moments of love—the photos—was not enough and we needed something more—writing.

We chose fourteen of the forty-odd photos and agreed that each would write separately, in total freedom, never show the other anything until it was done, or even change a word. The rule was strictly observed until the end.

There was only one exception. When we started to take these photos, I was undergoing treatment for breast cancer. While writing, I very quickly felt the necessity of evoking the other scene playing itself out inside my body, absent from the photographs—the blurred and stupefying ("Is it really me this is happening to?") struggle between life and death. I mentioned it to M. Like me, he was unable to ignore this aspect, which had been an essential part of our relationship for months. It was the only time we talked about the content of our "compositions," a spontaneous, provisional name for our project, corresponding (in both senses of the word) to what they were to us.

I cannot define the value or the interest of our undertaking. In a way, it belongs to the same frenzy for turning life into images that is increasingly characteristic of our age. Whether through photographs, or writing, we strove each time to give greater reality to moments of pleasure that were fleeting and impossible to represent. To capture the unreality of sex in the reality of what it leaves behind. The highest degree of reality, however, will only be attained if these written photos are transformed into other scenes in the reader's memory or imagination.

Cergy, October 22, 2004

In the photo, all we see of M., who is standing, is the part of his body between the bottom of his gray sweater with its wide cable ribs, level with the top of his auburn bush, and the middle of his thighs, over which his underwear—black boxer shorts with "Dim" in big white letters—has been lowered. The sex, seen in profile, is erect. The light from the flash illuminates the veins and makes a drop of sperm glisten at the tip of the glans, like a bead. The shadow of the erect penis is projected onto the books in the bookcase that occupies the entire right part of the photo. The names of the authors and titles can be read in large type: Lévi-Strauss, Martin Walser, *Cassandra*, *The Age of Extremes*. A hole can be seen at the bottom of the sweater.

I took this photo on February 11, after a quick lunch. I remember the bright sunshine in the room and his sex in the light. I had to take the RER into Paris, so we didn't have time to make love. The photo was the thing we did instead.

I can describe it, but I could not expose it to the eyes of others.

I realize that, in a way, it is the counterpart of Courbet's painting *The Origin of the World*, which for a long time I'd only ever seen in a photo in a magazine. It also has much in common with a scene I witnessed the summer I was twenty-three, at the Termini station, in Rome, as I was eating a hot dog, leaning against the open window of a train that was about to leave. Right across from me, in the train stopped on the other side of the platform, an erect penis, pulled free of a pair of trousers, was furiously stroked by the hand of a man hidden from the waist up by the blind he had lowered halfway in a first-class compartment.

I saw M.'s sex for the first time on the night of January 22 to 23, 2003, at my house, in the entrance hall, at the foot of the stairs leading up to the bedrooms. There is something extraordinary about the first appearance of the other's sex, the unveiling of what was hitherto unknown. So *that* is what we're going to live with, live our love with. Or not.

We'd had dinner together in a restaurant he knew well on rue Servandoni, near the Jardin du Luxembourg. He had just left the woman he'd been living with for several months. During the meal, I said, "I'd like to take you to Venice," and immediately added, "but I can't at the moment because I've got breast cancer, and I'm having an operation next week at the Institut Curie." He showed none of the signs—that almost imperceptible retraction, a sudden stiffening—through which even the most educated and composed people let their horror show in spite of themselves when I told them I had cancer. The only time he seemed disturbed was when I revealed that my new hairstyle, which he'd complimented many times, was a wig, and that I'd lost my hair as a result of chemotherapy. He was no doubt disappointed, even mortified to learn that the object of his admiration was a hairpiece.

(Now it occurs to me that I said to M., "I have breast cancer," in the same abrupt way I'd told a Catholic boy, in the sixties, "I'm pregnant and I want an abortion," in order to throw him into it, giving him no time to put up his guard and form an attitude in the face of an unbearable reality.)

After dinner, we went to a deserted bar on rue de Condé, with a big Buddha at the entrance. At one point, he said, as bluntly as the way in which I'd told him about my cancer, "I have an honest proposal for you: come spend the night with me at my hotel." I refused because I had an appointment with the anesthesiologist the following morning, and instead I invited him back to my house. On our way out, we put a coin in the basin at the Buddha's feet. We took the RER together. All I remember of the trip is a young and fashionably dressed black woman sitting next to us, talking on the phone with an earpiece and in a tone of argument that could only have meant she was speaking to someone close—husband, mother, child.

I didn't take off my wig in bed. I didn't want him to see my bald head. Chemotherapy had left my pubis bald, too. Near my armpit was a sort of protuberant beer cap, under the skin, a catheter implanted there at the start of treatment.[2]

He later admitted that he'd been startled by my sex, as naked as that of a little girl. He had never heard of this consequence of chemo—but who ever talks about it? I hadn't known either, until it happened to me. He didn't notice that evening that I had no eyelashes or eyebrows either, though their absence gave me the eerie gaze of a wax-faced doll.

At one point, staring at my chest, he asked me if the cancer was in my left breast. I was surprised. The right was visibly more swollen than the left because of the tumor. He could probably not imagine that the prettier of the two was the one with cancer.

There was a great sweetness to my stay at the Institut Curie for the surgery, which took place six days later. The tumor and lymph nodes were removed. The tissue analysis would determine whether the whole breast would have to be removed later. M. spent hours holding me in his arms. The smiles of the nurses and care assistants expressed approval. On Saturday it snowed. I could see the white roofs from my bed. I could hear the sounds of demonstrations against the war in Iraq from the boulevard Saint-Michel, and from the corridor the clear and

2 The central catheter, or "chamber," consists of a thin plastic tube inserted under the collarbone into the jugular vein, connected to a reservoir implanted under the skin, which is pierced at each chemotherapy session to introduce the substances that destroy the malignant cells. I'm describing this device with precision, because most people aren't familiar with it. I wasn't familiar with it either.

regular chime of the elevator stopping at my floor. I wrote in my journal that I felt infinitely happy.

Because of my totally smooth body he called me his mermaid-woman. The catheter like a growth protruding from my chest became a "supernumerary bone."

In the hallway

MARCH 6, 2003

at this time in my life

Clothing and shoes are scattered all the way down an entrance hallway with big pale tiles. In the foreground, on the right, is a red sweater or shirt and black tank top that appear to have been torn off and turned inside out in the same movement, resembling a low-cut bust with the arms cut off. A white label is clearly visible on the tank top. Further on is a pair of curled-up jeans with a black belt attached. To the left of the jeans, the red lining of a red jacket is spread out like a cloth for cleaning the floor. On top of that, a pair of blue-checkered boxer shorts and a white bra, one of whose straps is stretching out toward the jeans. Behind, a men's boot lies on its side next to a rumpled blue sock. Standing far apart and perpendicular to each other are two black high-heeled pumps. Even further away, protruding from under the radiator, is the black splotch of a sweater or skirt. On the other side, next to the wall, is a small black-and-white heap, impossible to identify. In the background we can discern the coatrack and the bottom of a trench coat whose belt is dangling down. The light of a flash illuminates the scene, whitening the tiles and the radiator, and making the leather of the pump we see in profile shimmer.

In another photo of the same scene, taken from a different angle, from a doorway, we see the other men's shoe and the other sock, alone at the bottom of a staircase.

I'm trying to describe the photo from two points of view, one past, one present. What I see now is not what I saw that morning when I came down the stairs before breakfast and stood in the hall with my hazy memory of the night before. It's a scene in which certain elements cannot be defined at first glance, and this place is different from the one I'm used to being in every day. It seems bigger to me, the tiles huge. To tell the truth, it is neither alien nor familiar, having simply undergone a distortion of its dimensions and a heightening of all its colors.

My first reaction is to try to discern beings in the shapes of objects, as in a Rorschach test, whose ink blots have been replaced by pieces of clothing and lingerie. I am no longer inside of the reality that gave rise to my emotion and to the photo I took that morning. It's my imagination that deciphers the photo, not my memory. I absolutely need to get it out of my field of vision, so that after a while, images of spring 2003 come back to me with a sort of delayed remembering, so that thought itself will be set in motion.

I found the date of the photo in my journal. On Thursday, March 6, I wrote: "He left in the hallway the composition formed by our shoes, our clothes all mixed together and piled here and there, mostly red and black. It was very beautiful. I took two photos."

Now, it seems to me that I have always wanted to preserve images of the devastated landscape that remains after love-making. I wonder why the idea of taking photos of it did not occur to me before, or why I never suggested it to any other man. Maybe I thought there was something vaguely shameful or unworthy about it. In a way, I felt it was less obscene—or now feel it is more acceptable—to photograph M.'s sex.

Perhaps, too, it is something I could only do with this man, and only at this time in my life.

For years, when I went to the library of the INRP, on rue d'Ulm, I had seen the Institut Curie across the street, with its adjoining garden of roses. I generally changed sidewalks before reaching the Institut. I would rush into the INRP with the sense of having escaped danger. I was temporarily safe. When I first walked through the glass door of the Institut Curie on the morning of October 3, 2002, I sensed that my reprieve had come to an end. I felt that breast cancer was something that was destined to happen to me like all the things that happen only to women, though neither my mother nor my grandmother ever had it, nor any of my aunts or cousins, and that in my family, I am the first, as in the case of higher education, as if I were blazing a trail.

I started throwing things away. The pack of hormone replacement therapy drugs, which I'd never use again. I told myself that I'd had my period for the last time in my life at the end of August, though I didn't know then that it would be the last. Papers, notes, lessons, old x-rays, shoes and clothes I hadn't worn for a long time.

When I bought the October issue of *Marie Claire*, I discovered that it was Breast Cancer Month. So, at least in this one way, I was keeping up with fashion. I remembered that I had bought the magazine for its "sex supplement" the summer before.

I called the town hall to buy a cemetery plot. The employee asked me how old I was. It could not be done before age seventy. Then she wanted to know why I wanted to buy a plot, and it amused me to say, "To prepare for the future!" It was still in the future, after all.

On the Internet, I pored over the countless sites devoted to breast cancer.

Whereas at an earlier time in my life, I'd seen the signs of jealousy everywhere, now I saw the signs of death. As I left the Leroy Merlin home improvement store, I saw an arrow pointing in the direction of the morgue; a gadget I'd received as a gift contained a tiny clock, and so on.

My aversion to housework became radical. The order and conservation of things seemed more absurd than ever. I wasn't going to add death to death.

I bought two pairs of shoes and two cashmere sweaters, telling myself it was a big expense, useless in my condition—but money was useless too.

At the Auber RER station, at the bottom of the escalator, I passed a gypsy woman holding out her hand, a child in her arms. I realized she was breastfeeding. Her breast was purple. I retraced my steps and gave her a coin. For the sake of mine.

I remembered Violette Leduc and looked up in a biography how long she'd survived with her breast cancer: seven years. That was enough time to write. I was looking for a literary form that would contain my whole life. It did not yet exist.

In the Métro, at the bank, I'd look at old women, their deep wrinkles, their drooping eyelids, and say to myself, "I'll never be old." It wasn't a sad thought, just surprising. I'd never had that thought before.

The thing that struck me most was the simplicity of it all.

As I crossed the threshold of the Institut Curie for the first time, Dante's phrase came back to me, "Abandon all hope, ye who enter here." But inside, on the contrary, I felt I was in a kind of ideal setting, unparalleled in our times, where smiling and attentive human beings give care and kindness to other destitute humans. Very quickly, without thinking about it, I took the signposted route from the Luxembourg RER station at the heart of the Latin Quarter, where among all the intersecting paths for learning, shopping, lovers' meetings, and tourism, there is one for cancer patients.

To say "I've got chemo tomorrow" became as natural as it was the year before to say "I've got a hair appointment."

the hallway composition

From the flash lighting up the scene, I know it was A. who took the photo.

The artificial lighting makes it impossible to tell whether it is morning or evening. Nor is there any way of dating the photo exactly, apart from the note on the back, <N° 8> PS CERGY MAR 2003. For a long time I attributed its authorship to myself, convinced that it was me who had initiated the practice of photographing the scattering of our clothes after lovemaking. There's a probable reason for this distortion of memory: the shared, almost simultaneous desire to preserve a trace of the hours that had just passed. To tell myself today that this photo was the first of many has no reality in itself. If we spread out all these pictures on a table, this one would have no more value as an incipit than any other.

Our clothes are strewn all over the floor. A.'s clothes, apart from her high-heeled pumps, which have remained upright, are so tangled up with each other, in both the foreground and the background, that all you can make out is a white bra. Thus abandoned, they surround my uniform of the time—jeans, boots, a red shirt. They enclose, almost embrace it.

When I first saw this puzzle made of cloth and leather, I was struck by the dazzling beauty of the scene. The trouser leg turned inside out, underwear in a knot, shoelaces half untied all spoke to me of the power of the act and of the moment. There were traces of a struggle and, concentrated in a few square meters, sex and violence—the east and west of the spectrum of passions.

I would have liked not to touch anything, to leave each object where it was. We had made love, and several hours had passed. The visual memory we would retain, along with other memories of the same kind, over nights, weeks, months, would form an entity, resonant but indistinct. I would reconstruct in A.'s bedroom an embrace that had in fact taken place in her office; I would situate a CD we'd listened to in the autumn as having been played in the spring. Perhaps it was because I was certain, at the time, that one day I would forget the look on her face when she came, the inflections in her voice when she hummed along with the radio, the way she sucked my cock, and the movement of her body when she was on top—all these things that cannot be photographed—and because, like her, I felt the imperious need to capture on film the exact location of our clothes, tangible evidence of what we had just experienced. Without touching or moving anything. As the cops would do after a murder.

Week after week, the photos accumulated, several dozen in all. The spontaneous act of taking photos became a matter of ritual. But always, at the moment when I collected my things and destroyed that harmony, my heart sank, as if each time I were desecrating the relics of a sacred place. To us it was as beautiful as a work of art, as remarkable for the play of colors as for the interaction between the different fabrics as if, though immobile for the moment, they were preparing to creep toward each other and perpetuate our gestures. The crime lay not in what we'd done, but in the action of undoing it.

Later, when we finally saw the negatives developed, the expression that came to our minds to describe this first photo was *the hallway composition.*

Room 223 of the Hotel Amigo

BRUSSELS, MARCH 10

a resemblance with shorn women

The breakfast table in front of the unmade bed. The coffee pot and a bread basket with the remaining toast and pastries. On top of the sheets, a small black heap, the silk blouse given to me by a friend before my operation at the Curie, and something red, maybe one of M.'s shirts. On the right, appearing almost black in the shadows, red roses in a vase. Behind, the half-open window.

The photo was taken on Monday morning, shortly before we left the room. It's not a postcoital landscape, just the image of a room where you've lived for three days and that you will probably never see again and whose details will mostly be forgotten. Just as I've forgotten almost everything—except where the bed stood in relation to the window and the television—about the room where I stayed with Z. in this same hotel in February 1986, and two months later, my mother suddenly died. That she was still alive when I first came to this hotel seems to me incredible—that means there was a time when I could see her, hear her voice, touch her, when she wasn't there above me. I can't imagine that time. Maybe it's because M. also stayed at the Hotel Amigo in 2001, when he was mad with grief over the death of his own mother, three months earlier. I can't picture us in the same place, me with my mother alive and he with his mother dead, whereas their deaths are fourteen years apart, and there is such a vast expanse of my mother's absence behind me.

The red roses are the ones he gave me on Saturday afternoon. He'd been gone for over an hour and I thought he'd gone out to phone the woman he left. When I opened the door and saw him with the bouquet, I was ashamed of my suspicions, as if the two actions—phoning another woman and giving me flowers—were incompatible. But maybe he phoned *and* bought flowers.

It was in the bathroom of this room that I showed myself to him with my bald head for the first time. We'd been together for seven weeks. He told me that it suited me. He noticed that my hair was starting to grow back, the faintest white and black baby-chick fuzz. I had not yet noticed it.

I've seen a lot of photos of women whose heads were shaved at the time of Liberation. I was even asked one day to comment on some of these photos and I agreed, but the project didn't come to fruition due to lack of funding. It gave me a strange feeling to resemble the shorn women now.

I'd lost my hair in two weeks. One night, it seemed to turn into quills lodged in my tight-stretched scalp. When I woke up, it was falling out in handfuls and I began to pile it into a large envelope. Before I was completely bald, I went into a "hair replacement" shop on rue Danielle-Casanova, located (so I realized when I got there) directly across from the hotel where I'd met a man a few times in the afternoon in the spring of 1984, and which, at the time, I'd thought was a brothel. I chose a long blonde wig with copper highlights, close to my old hairstyle. It slipped easily over my head like a woolly hat, could be detangled with a brush and washed in the sink with shampoo. I had every reason to be pleased. At first I was afraid it would be obvious or blow off in the wind. After that, I forgot about it.

Although it is a prop,[3] it does not appear in any of the photos. Even after Brussels, for a long time I only removed it at bedtime, with the light off. I'd throw it to the bottom of the bed and as soon as I woke up, search around for it and pull it back on my head.

Before leaving the hotel room, I looked out the window at the little square and the two streets leading off it on either side of a building that tapered to a point and flared out behind, like an ocean liner cleaving through the sea, a perspective of converging lines common in big European cities, Paris, Rome,

3 Actually, it's more a sign, of cancer, as the headscarf is a sign of the Islamic religion. Hence the abandonment of both as purely feminine fashion accessories, which is what they were until the invention of chemotherapy and the development of Islam.

etc., which I always find moving. I wondered if we would ever return to Brussels together.

A hotel room, with its double impermanence, temporal and spatial, is for me a place where the pain of love is felt most acutely. At the same time, I've always had the impression that making love in a hotel is *without consequence* because there, in a sense, you are nobody. For the same reason, it is probably easier to die in a hotel room, like Pavese or Marco Pantani.

Annie Lennox

I'd gone to buy roses on boulevard Anspach. It was a cool, gray afternoon, a Saturday. A. had stayed at the hotel and was uneasy, probably imagining that I was going to take advantage of the time to get back in touch with my ex, whom I'd left on January 20. I knew A. was worried, and in truth, it didn't really bother me, knowing I'd be returning with an armful of flowers for the first time since we'd met.

The roses are there, in the shadow on the right side of the photo. The bedroom window overlooks a little square where the Amigo's entrance is located. In the space of two years, the hotel has had a complete makeover, the Louis XV–style gilt and furnishings replaced by a drab brown '50s décor, whose tones remind me of the Telefunken hi-fi equipment of my childhood. The new owner, the Rocco Forte chain, preferred to demolish the original layout, reducing the ceiling height to increase the number of rooms. In the lobby, we meet businessmen and women, who all look very much alike, civilized, with no rough edges. On the walls of the bar on the ground floor, autographed photos of writers still have pride of place. A last vestige. An anachronism.

Since our arrival on Friday, we've been going from place to place in the pouring rain—Uccle, the Bourse, the rue du Midi, the rue du Marché aux Poulets, the Métropole bar, the place de Brouckère—Brussels as I've always known it, not really hostile, just *reticent.*

I was eight when my parents left Brussels. De Gaulle had just died. By the end of the school year, our bags were packed. I did not return until twelve years later. Not a very good memory. Lots of tears. Still, the return visits add up. In November 2000, my mother dies. Three months later, as if by reflex, I'm back in Brussels. I go with a friend. I have a bit of money so we stay at the Amigo. It rains nonstop and the cold drives us to spend hours in restaurants. I drink a lot. We take a few photos. When I come across the pictures later in Paris, for the first time since my mother's death, I see my face, my features, which are those of a punch-drunk boxer.

For three months, I have not replied to a single message of condolence. One evening, however, at the writing desk in the hotel room, I compose a letter to the woman writer with whom I've maintained an irregular correspondence for the past two years. It is a long letter, six or seven pages, in which I tell her what I am unable to confide to my friends, about the loss, the emptiness, the disappearance of meaning in everything. On my return to Paris, I find her reply, in which she expresses surprise at seeing the letterhead from the Hotel Amigo, where she once stayed in 1986, shortly before learning that her own mother had died.

We had Brussels in common without knowing it. To go there for our first trip together seemed to us only natural.

What I particularly like about this photo is the mess. We've just finished breakfast, the sheets are rumpled, the pillows wilted. On the bed, which is just in front of the desk, is what is probably A.'s black silk shirt, worn in two other photos where she also wears her wig. It is during this trip that she shows me her scalp for the first time, where new hair has grown, very short. I think it suits her. That she looks like Annie Lennox, who is performing in Brussels at this time, and whose posters are popping up everywhere. I love to stroke her brand new, post-chemo hair, a very soft down, a second birth. I say that I'd like her to go out that way and finally get rid of her artificial headdress—here, she's unlikely to see anyone she knows. But she refuses, on the grounds that it is cold outside.

Brussels is also the first place we appear together in a photo. Like thousands of tourists, we ask a couple to take a photo of us on the Grand-Place. The photo is poorly framed. But my boxer face has disappeared.

A few days after our return to France, during a quarrel, A. will say, "The happiness of Brussels is over."

The shoe in the living room

MARCH 15

a secret

On the wooden floor, very striking in close-up, is the same men's boot as in the first photo: Doc Martens–style, black leather, gaping like an open mouth, with hooks for tying the laces crisscross. It is obvious from the deep creases in the leather upper and tongue that it's a shoe that has been worn a great deal. The toe presses down on a white-patterned red lace bra that is twisted on itself. The untied bootlaces trail over the bra. Behind the shoe is the leg of a pair of jeans to which the belt remains attached. It bisects a square of light-colored suede, like a piece of skin, which probably has the brand name stamped upon it.

The light from the flash gives the boot a devouring look. Makes me want to cut it out of the photo and paste it up somewhere as an illustration of male domination, though in reality my relationship with M. in no way corresponds to this scene that is staged by the objects themselves.

From one photo to the next, it's almost always these shoes that appear, with their laces more or less untied and the gape-mouthed look of an old hobnail boot at the end of a fishing line in cartoons of the last century. These are the shoes that M. most often wears, broken down and misshapen. The system of lacing forces us to interrupt the flow of our caresses, compels desire to wait while he takes them off. I have a persistent image of him trapped by his jeans, pulled down to the middle of his legs, and of his efforts to pull the boots off, one after the other.

Of all the things abandoned on the floor after lovemaking, shoes are the most moving—overturned, or upright but heading in opposite directions, or adrift on top of a heap of clothes but still far apart. The distance between them, when it can be seen in the photo, reflects the force with which they were flung off. More often than not, they are isolated, like shoes found in parking lots, or on sidewalks, that make you wonder who got rid of them and why. Unlike other pieces of clothing, which in a photo become abstract forms, shoes retain the shape of a body part. They are the element that conveys presence in the *realest* possible way. They are the most human of accessories.

In a short story by de Maupassant, a maid admits that she slept with the farmer, her master, simply by saying, "We mixed our sabots." Nobody says "sabots" now. One day, M. and I will no longer mix ours.

The thought that he has begun to write about these photos, these remnants of a night, fills me with a kind of excitement I've never felt before, as much intellectual as physical. It's a secret we share, a sort of new erotic practice.

I feel there's nothing we could do together that would be better than this, an act of writing at once united and disjointed. Sometimes it also frightens me. To open up your writing space is more violent than to open up your sex. I wonder what unconscious strategy may already be at work in me to ensure that he gets no space. Making words and sentences unyielding, paragraphs as impossible to move as the stone my body sometimes became when I was little, while the walls of the bedroom endlessly receded, symptoms that I later learned with surprise but no fear, when studying philosophy, were those of schizophrenia.

combat gear

A men's shoe tramples a bra. Or rather, the toe of the shoe is pressing down on it, and the movement behind the photo can almost be felt—that of the heel swinging right and left in a gesture of fury and disgust—and it's no longer a bra but the hornet crushed on the kitchen floor one summer evening. Nor are these the sleek pair of ankle boots spotted in a shop window in the Forum des Halles four years earlier. Since then, I must have worn them three hundred days a year. My friends can't imagine me with anything else on my feet, to the point of wondering: Does the guy actually have the cash to buy a new pair of kicks? Kicks, shoes, boots, stompers, Chelsea boots, lace-up boots, Docs—when I talk about them I just say "my boots." The leather is worn out, the black paint on the hooks has rubbed off in places, exposing the original brass. The way they are now, gaping and abandoned, they have the miserable grace of the hobnail boots that the Pieds Nickelés pull from the Seine at the end of their fishing lines on days when they're having no luck in the old comic strip.

The symbolism of the photo is so obvious that you could legitimately doubt that the arrangement is just a matter of chance. But I can still see myself at the moment I discovered this detail, smiling at how faithfully chance had reproduced a conventional image of the male throttling the eternal feminine with the single, black and imperious pressure of the shoe. The shoelaces trail over the bra on either side, as if to take hold of it, twirl it around, and make it repeat the light dance it had done at the moment I unfastened the hooks and it fell.

It's the boot for the right foot, the one used to kick a ball. I have on several occasions, with A., extolled the virtues of a good kick in the balls if you are being attacked. I bought my first boots of this type, Montanas, in Montpellier, during the Atlanta games. A year later, I fell asleep on the last train back to my mother's house in Val-d'Oise. I woke up in Orry-la-Ville, twenty kilometers from home. No taxis. The station was in the middle of the woods. As there were no roads near the railway line, I found myself walking on the ballast, between the rails, listening to the noise of the nighttime freight trains, dreading being crushed under their wheels. My boots were solid but ill-suited to what I was putting them through—my boots, my last stronghold. I feared rape more than anything else, punches in the face, or even wanton murder committed just for fun. I didn't meet anyone that night. My mother, used to seeing me come home late, didn't hear anything when I came in and went to bed like a good boy. The next day at noon, I looked at my things, my "combat gear." Smashed soles, lacerated leather—my boots were ruined.

A. is tall. For months, I didn't want her to see me in flat shoes. When I was on the street with her, I always tried to walk on the high side of the pavement so that I could put my hand on her shoulder in a protective, dominant, eminently, obviously masculine posture. I'd grown so acclimated by the women who'd passed through my life until then to having to adopt the tired old getups of the Male: a plaid shirt so I would look like a lumberjack, a baseball cap so I would look American, a three-day beard for a virile look, skateboarder pants for a trendy look, jeans that hugged my balls to make up for the non-hugging of my nonexistent buttocks. Only my boots survived these attempts to pass myself off as something I wasn't, with the undesired effect of forcing me, just as I was about to make love, to struggle through four rows of hooks, unlace my clodhoppers in semidarkness, overwhelmed by clumsiness in the excitement of the moment, during which interval the said excitement had ample time to subside, reducing my sex to its limp everyday demeanor. Later, whether I was at home in Paris, or in Cergy, the first thing I did when I walked through the door was to put on loafers. The fragility of desire. Much better to permanently adopt the kind of outfits used by quick-change artists. Snap fasteners, Velcro, zippers.

The kitchen in the morning

SUNDAY, MARCH 16

the big holiday

On the right in the photo, light wood cupboards, a white dishwasher. On the countertop, on either side of the gleaming sink, trays leaning up against the wall, a chopping board, various electrical appliances, a bottle of bleach with a green cap, another of green plant fertilizer, a packet of Whiskas, a potbellied kettle with a black handle shaped like a gear lever, a cast-iron casserole, a dish with food in it, an open Tupperware container with a red lid next to it, as if waiting to receive the leftovers from the dish, a dish towel. The ceramic tiled floor a sort of '50s blue-and-beige checker-board. Next to the cupboard from which it was taken, a full trash can with orange peel pressed down on top of the trash. Touching the bin, the dark puddle of a thick garment stretches out on the checkerboard tiles like a bearskin. Next to it, a white slipper with something written on it. At the foot of the dishwasher, a small heap of crumpled, reddish-purple fabric, and the other slipper whose tip rests on a sort of blue-and-white rag. Behind the dark heap is a chair in a strange position, perpendicular to the table on which sits a large microwave oven, as if someone had been listening to it like a radio, with their ear pressed against it. The sun coming in through the window at the back draws slashes of light across the bearskin.

In another vertical shot of the same scene, the light, more intense, illuminates the dishwasher, the countertop to the left of the sink with the fertilizer and the bleach, and projects an image of the window, long and white, on the tiled floor.

Nothing has been put away here, neither the remains of the meal nor those of love. Two kinds of disorder.

It took me a long time to identify our dressing gowns, his of dark-green terry, mine of plum-colored synthetic silk, and to make out what was written on the slippers: “Hôtel Amigo.” I no longer know what we had eaten the night before, the remains of which can be seen in the dish. Nor do I remember anything of our caresses or our pleasure.

There is nothing in the photo of the smells of the kitchen in the morning, a mixture of coffee and toast, cat food and March air. None of the noises either, the regular sound of the fridge starting up, perhaps the neighbor’s lawn mower, a plane from Roissy. Just the light falling forever on the tiles, the oranges in the bin, the green cap on the bottle of bleach. All the photos are mute, especially those taken in the morning sun.

I was able to put a date to the photo using my journal: the last Sunday before the United States attacked Iraq. Everyone was waiting for the war, which had been planned for months. Millions of people around the world were marching to stop it from happening, but it continued to advance like a giant shadow over sun-scorched earth. I felt guilty for not having taken as violent a stand against the war as I had in 1991, simply hanging a white banner on my balcony as a sign of pacifist opposition, a gesture that was not as widespread in France, and whose only effect may have been to make me look crazy in the eyes of my neighbors.

One morning, I turned on the radio, and there it was: a distant horror that I could feel only through my love affair with M. It was a very hot day, the sun imperturbable, and I thought: "Another beautiful spring." I was free of all obligations, even writing. All I had to do was live out this story with M. Waste time. The big holiday from life. The great cancer holiday.

At last, I was allowed to shirk my duties of politeness, and not reply to letters or emails. People's insistence, when I refused an invitation to a debate or a reading, seemed outrageous to me, a form of persecution. Of course, my reaction had to do with the fact of being ill, of which they were unaware. Had I told them, they would have apologized profusely. But to feel they were ascribing my refusal to a whim, taking it as a personal affront (that is, thinking only of themselves) made me intractable. I was done with other people's vanity. I was unreachable.

I had told very few people about my cancer. I wanted no part of the kind of sympathy which could never conceal, whenever it was expressed, the obvious fact that for others I'd become someone else. I could see my future absence in their eyes.

They had no idea that it was their death I was seeing, which was every bit as certain as my own. And I had an advantage over them, which was that I knew it.

One day, he said to me, "You only got cancer so you could write about it." I felt that in a way he was right, but up until that point, I'd been unable to come to terms with this. It was only when I started writing about these photos that I was able to do so, as if writing about the photos authorized me to write about the cancer. As if there were a link between the two.

In another sense, he was wrong. I don't expect life to bring me *subjects* but *unknown structures* for writing. The thought "I only want to write the texts that only I can write" refers to texts whose very form is provided by the reality of my life. I could never have foreseen the text we are writing. Though it definitely came from life. Conversely, the writing under the photos, in multiple fragments which will themselves be broken up by those of M., as yet unknown, give me (among other things) the chance to create *a minimal narrative* out of this reality.

pace

More than the clothes themselves, what strikes me is the light coming through the kitchen windows. A white, monochrome screen for all the events that punctuate early 2003, scrolling one after another. The first morning after our first night together, A. shows me the white sheet she has hung on the front of the house, under her bedroom balcony, to protest the impending American invasion of Iraq. Tattered by the elements, this shabby but highly visible banner dominates the valley below where a big new house stands alone. I tell myself that A. must be taken for the *pasionaria* of this bourgeois neighborhood where no one speaks to each other.

But then, at the beginning of May, we set off for Venice, where a myriad of five-colored flags flutter from the balconies of palaces and the most modest of dwellings, all emblazoned with the same word, PACE. Peace. In Venice I cease to show amusement toward something that I had mistaken four months earlier for an eccentricity.

Hidden in the shadows, our clothes are barely recognizable, except for the Amigo mules. The rest—the bread basket to the left of the microwave, the oranges on top, the bin full of fruit rinds, the trays set vertically behind the faucet of the sink, an open Tupperware container—are only illustrations of everyday life, the remnants of our breakfasts behind which lies the essence: our uninterrupted conversations, the transistor radio that disseminates new litanies, month after month—the invasion of Iraq by the United States in March, the bombings from an altitude of six thousand meters, the fall of Baghdad, the first terrorist attacks. The horror at the other end of our love, as if the outside world had always to be there, beyond the kitchen window.

The kitchen in Cergy. My favorite room. Because of the morning sun that devours the tiles. Because of A.'s gestures as she is making dinner. Because of the first time I offered to help her peel potatoes, my embarrassment at the idea of these beginnings of a life together, considering my abortive, failed attempts to blend in, through insignificant actions with a socially acceptable, recognized model, "the couple," an entity A. hates and which I regard with a mixture of envy and repulsion. Because of the pleasure of looking at her ass when she's cooking, and the shame of feeling a mixture of machismo and lust in those moments. Because of the music coming from another room, the sound at full volume but distorted by the hallway. Because of the never-changing path taken by Kyo the cat, who reigns over the premises, bursts through the half-open window and, like an actress climbing the steps of the Palais des Festivals on the night of a screening, invades the countertop to receive her due: chicken cutlets and raw chicken livers. Because of nights when the pale moonlight licks the ground and fills the whole main floor. Because of more tragic aspects too: shouting matches in the middle of the night, those moments when we cease to understand each other, and with our butts parked on the dishwasher, wearing our nasty insomniac faces, we rip into each other for a while, on account of a reproach, a bout of jealousy, a lapse in attention or desire, with the deep and single-minded yearning to fight to the finish with verbal violence, words that wound, and sex, perhaps, as the ultimate mode of communication.

Cergy, its kitchen, its overheated rooms and isolation, a micro-universe that kept me removed both from a current event perceived as minor—the war in Iraq—and the final spasms of the life I'd just left. The breakup that preceded my meeting with A., though it plagued the first months of our relationship, today appears, via these photos, as a form of prehistory—the accidental foundations of that which led me to her, to her bed—led to our bewitched faces and revelatory mornings. Waking up beside each other with no clothes or makeup on, breath sour and eyes full of sleep, can be a point of no return: you either rush into the shower and set your sights on going home as quickly as possible, or you stay for breakfast.

In the office

APRIL 5

for what revelation?

On the floor in the foreground, on the carpet that forms a sort of narrow green corridor between the white baseboard of a wall and the vertical side of a desk, are several sheets of paper, overlapping and in disarray, covered with handwriting. One sheet has slid halfway under the desk. Further on is a multiple socket with three wires running out of it, two on the floor and the other spiraling up toward the desktop, connected to a lamp that cannot be seen. At the far end, a dozen felt-tip pens and pencils in various colors, fanning out in all directions, one on top of the other like pickup sticks, next to the overturned cup that used to hold them. It's obvious that all these objects have fallen off the desk where they had been.

This photo is one of a group of three taken the same evening, in the same room. Unlike the two others, which show the chaos of our scattered clothes, this one shows only the objects that we knocked off the desk without noticing. We had dined at the Auberge Ravoux in Auvers-sur-Oise, beneath the room where Van Gogh once lay dying, whose owner at the time had the thoughtful habit of showing guests around, free of charge, after they had eaten the succulent leg of lamb, roasted for five hours, and a creamy chocolate mousse.

The light of a halogen lamp at maximum power, combined with that of the flash, brings out the whiteness of the pages and makes it possible to discern the layout of the sentences, the erasures and the words written on top in darker ink. I would like to read what is written. In all photos and postcards that contain an advertisement, a book cover, a newspaper, or anything written, I always try to make out the words, as a truer sign of the times than the rest of the image. In a prewar photo of my father in his Sunday best, together with an unknown communicant and a child I know to be my sister, who died at the age of six, there is a poster on the wall whose headlines I can read: THE HIGH COST OF LIVING—SALARY HIKES—THE FORTY-HOUR WEEK.

Here, in spite of my best efforts, I cannot read the writing, even with a magnifying glass.

I can't remember what I was writing at that time. But of this I am sure: the night we took the photos, if I'd had to choose between making love with M. and preserving my pages of notes, it is not them I would have chosen.

I thought, "He makes me live *above* cancer."

One night, at the beginning of our relationship, as we were lying side by side, unable to sleep, he said, of the woman he'd left, "Do you think I've become indifferent to her?" I got out of bed and went downstairs to the kitchen. The next afternoon, I had to go to the Institut Curie, where the surgeon who had performed my surgery a fortnight earlier was going to tell me whether the removal of the tumor was enough or whether my whole breast had to be removed. Sitting in a chair in the kitchen at two in the morning, I told myself that the pain caused by M. was worse, at that moment, than not yet knowing whether I was done for or not.

Every man I've been involved with seems to have brought me some kind of revelation, different each time. The difficulty for me in doing without a man has less to do with purely sexual need than with my desire to know. To know what, I cannot say. I still don't know what revelation M. was supposed to offer me.

sanctuary

The objects that fell to the floor came from on top of her worktable: sheets of paper on which A. had made notes, and further away, a china mug surrounded by its contents: felt-tip markers and pencils spread out on the floor like a game of pickup sticks. We'd made love on the desk, and sent flying most of what was on it. Immediately I wanted to take photos of the sacking of the sanctuary. In January, when A. showed me her house, I logically expected her to forbid me access to this room. She didn't. It's a room like any other, with a bookcase, family photos, and a telephone. The window looks out on tall trees—there is no horizon, no distractions. Yet I'd been irresistibly drawn to the desk itself. Not because a fair number of her books had been conceived there, but because the piece of furniture itself seemed propitious to writing. A few days later, while A. was at the hospital, I sat down there one evening to write to her. Also to see how it felt. It didn't feel like anything. I was simply happy at the idea of giving her my letter the next day. There was snow outside, and twenty kilometers away, my parents' house, damp and unheated, and even further away, A. alone at the Curie. Visiting hours ended at 8 p.m. The nurses and care assistants took a positive view of my presence, they must have found us endearing as a new couple.

For several long weeks, I had her desk before me, with the pale green folders that protect her works in progress always in the same place. Also in plain view, on the bottom shelves of the bookcase, were the original manuscripts of her published works. I never looked at them, I wasn't even tempted.

Nonetheless, on the night when the photo was taken, her forgetting for a while the thing for which she is socially recognized gave me pleasure, as did baptizing this sacred space (which she may have done with someone else before me) by depositing my bare buttocks upon it and witnessing the spectacle of its destruction by our arms and thighs, which temporarily laid waste to what, at that moment, had ceased to have value.

If the image were enlarged, we could probably decipher A.'s handwriting on the pages strewn on the carpet. What would we find? Notes scribbled in haste? During a conference, by way of introduction, the director of the Institut Français de Valence screened a profile of ten or so minutes long, filmed entirely at the house in Cergy and broadcast in France in June 2000 as part of the Histoires d'écrivains series. In the main, it shows A. writing at her desk, the kind of scene that unfailingly comes up when writers are presented in their natural element, like an endangered animal species. I remember A's fear that when the image of the page was projected on the big screen, we might see what she was really writing: a short rambling passage in which she expressed her desire for this hackneyed scene to end. Photographers and television viewers are always very partial to these moments described as candid—Verlaine at a bistro table in front of a glass of absinthe, Kennedy supposedly perusing files of great importance in the Oval Office while little John-John slides under the table to play, simply because he's a kid and the table is just the right height.

Red shawl

APRIL 12 OR 20

like stains

A colorful tangle of clothes, half on the parquet floor and half on a rug at the foot of a solid piece of furniture in light-colored wood, of which only the bottom of the closed doors can be seen. Next to it is a chair, pushed back from a table that cannot be seen, over which a big red shawl is draped. Another chair sits across from it, also pushed away from the table.

At the foot of the chair with the shawl, on the carpet, is a dainty black sandal with a pointed closed toe and straps around the back that leave the heel bare. So it was one of those April evenings that were already so warm. The other sandal is quite far away, on the parquet, as if it had stepped over the bundle of clothes. In the foreground is M.'s big shoe, hanging open. The other lies perpendicular to the high-heeled sandal on the parquet. In this hodgepodge of clothes, where light hues alternate with dark, I think I recognize a blue shirt of M.'s, a black skirt, black tights turned inside out with a shock of white gusset, M.'s beige trousers, also inside out, his blue socks and Dim boxers, black with white stripes. Whether or not these things are fashionable, expensive or cheap, is unimportant. As in a still life, all that counts are the shapes and colors, the draping of the shawl, the blue of the socks in counterpoint to that of the shirt, the white of the boxers' waistband emphasizing that of the leather interior of the black shoes.

The stability, the solidity of the furniture, the clean lines drawn by the carpet and by the parallel slats of the parquet—something heavy and orderly, immutable—contrasts with the disorder and fragility of the skins cast off on the floor, accentuates the precariousness of the scene that had needed, as usual, to be speedily erased, once the photo had been taken.

A woman, Ninon B., sent me four photos taken in this same living room, in 1970, when she occupied this house that later became mine. We see her daughter in a tutu moving gracefully between gilded armchairs. I recognized the wooden floor. It is the one in the shawl photo, absolutely identical. So, in the place where a teenage girl danced thirty years ago, we fell asleep naked amid scattered clothes, heedless of the discomfort, like little cats who drop from exhaustion anywhere at all after playing. Among the many beliefs that I do not wish to part with is that houses retain the memory of everything that has happened inside them. Why wouldn't they? According to an article in *Le Monde*, geneticists have confirmed that a woman's womb retains an *imprint* of all the children, whether born or aborted, that have developed there.

At the time this photo was taken, I was helping M. to empty out his parents' house, which was going to be sold. Concealed at the very back of a garden, masked by reed fencing in Villiers-le-Bel, small and dark, it resembled a mausoleum. M.'s mother, who died in 2000, had not changed anything or thrown anything away since the death of M.'s father fifteen years earlier. The shelves were filled to bursting with books and the closets with clothes. M.'s mother's dresses, suits, and coats, jammed together on hangers, remained suffused with the smell of the eau de cologne she used to excess, combined with the smell of the house itself: wood fires and damp walls that no form of heating could dry. I stood before them, not daring to touch anything. They were vivid, multiple images of a woman I'd never met, and of whom, apart from the photos, I would never know anything other than these dresses, handbags, and shoes. M. didn't seem to be able to touch them either. We left all the clothes behind, taking only the objects and the books.

Now I feel as if, by dint of having sorted and put in boxes, along with M., the things that had belonged to his mother, her cookbooks and gardening books, the works of the writer she loved most, Colette, her household linens, her sewing and drawing materials, without ever having met her, I'd gotten to know her all the same. And, more disturbingly, as if she had gotten to know me too.

I realize that I am fascinated by photos in the same way I've been fascinated, since childhood, by blood, semen, and urine stains on sheets, or old mattresses, discarded on sidewalks; by the stains of wine or food embedded in the wood of sideboards, the stains of coffee or greasy fingers on old letters—the most material and organic kinds of stains. I realize that I expect the same thing from writing. I want words to be like stains you cannot tear yourself away from.

I've heard that gypsy brides and grooms in Kosovo are in the habit of exposing the wedding sheet on which they have attempted to draw designs using blood and semen. The guests take the sheet, smear the blood with wine, and in this way create other compositions. I wonder if they photograph them.

The red shawl is for late evenings, which are always a little chilly in Cergy. On the right is a round table, which cannot be seen in the photo. That is where we eat dinner when we've decided not to go out. Again, it's part of the ritual, in the sense that from the first night on, we have split time into pieces. As if our days were numbered. As if to create a series of perfect moments (the aperitif at the little table in the living room, the preparation of the meal, the spreading of the tablecloth, the arrangement of the crockery and candlesticks, the choosing of the wine), small bubbles inside which the tragedy of events in our respective lives is at once trivialized and denied the right to linger. Between one bubble and the next, death eventually loosened its grip. Not very persistent, death. And yet, and yet.

On January 20, after leaving the woman I lived with, our apartment and my job as a sales assistant, all at the same time, I took a room in a hotel in Saint-Germain-des-Prés. My parents' house is uninhabitable, the boiler having exploded due to freezing temperatures. Since the beginning of the month, it has been extremely cold in Paris. I tell myself that I will stay at the hotel for a few days. I am hibernating. I call A., whom I am supposed to see the following week, to bring the appointment forward. We settle on January 22. And then things do an about-face, for reasons I still find hard to decipher, and which I never really try to go back and review, because it was such a bumpy, troubled period, lived in total unconsciousness. So I'm having dinner with this very beautiful woman, who tells me as we are eating the appetizer that she has cancer. At the time, it makes no difference, and it is at that moment, it seems to me, that we spontaneously create our first bubble, from which the illness is not only not excluded but in which it is *incorporated* from the outset. For months, we live together as a threesome, death, A., and me. Our companion was intrusive. It continually claimed its right to be there, in the pouch of liquid stuck to A.'s belly during the periods of chemotherapy, in the catheter under her collarbone, on her nipple burned by radiotherapy, on the blackened border of her gums and all over her body that was now completely hairless, in her complexion as waxy as that of a figure in the Musée Grévin, a uniformity of tone that I had seen only once before in my life, on the seventh floor of the medical school on rue des Saints-Pères, where cadavers await dissection. Intrusive, but powerless against our love. I know it's almost too beautiful to believe, the old myth of love's victory over death, but that's the way it is. And besides, death is still there. A.'s hair has grown back, but you have to wait five years after the operation to be sure of being "out of the woods."

Our meeting may have been improbable, but that we endured was equally so. Often, especially on long walks along the beach at Trouville at low tide, I think about the fact that neither she nor I should be there. I look at the woman walking next to me, this laughing woman, so alive, whose birth was contingent on the death of her sister, and whose life, for a time, hung by a thread. It's a strange feeling. Like being weightless ghosts, accidental spectators.

Kitchen

APRIL 17

three million breasts

The kitchen again. The clothes are scattered in four heaps of different sizes on the yellow-and-gray checkerboard of tiles that occupies almost the entire photo. In the foreground, the biggest heap, which covers an area of six by five squares, consists of a skirt and a gray suit jacket turned inside out on its shiny lining. Underneath is a blue shirt. Three dark cavities amid the folds of fabric make hollows in the lining that evoke a gas mask. The usual big Doc Martens lies next to the shirt, on its side. A long dark gray stocking wriggles out of the heap onto the tiles. Next to the shoe are the cups of a flower-patterned bra, delicately laid flat, and a pair of underpants, also with flowers. Above, on the right, is a small red heap—a sweater with the sleeve folded back. On the left, jeans with a belt, and a gap filled by a T-shirt. The other Doc is there, tipped on its side. An isolated sock. At the very back, between the feet of the old sewing machine: a small, closed bin bag and an empty rosé bottle.

It is a morning photo, without sun. In my journal: "This morning, pleasure in the kitchen."

In all the photos, our clothes—suit, shirts—lie on the floor, showing off the things we hardly ever see: the labels with the washing instructions, linings, the gusset on the tights. They were flung off in the urgency of desire, at the risk of being damaged and stained, with no concern for their market value: for a moment, no one is *thinking of the cost.* They have fulfilled their seductive function and anticipate the other that will be theirs one day: to be used as rags to polish furniture or shoes.

(I hear the words of my mother, *that child does not think of the cost of anything* and *slattern!* Words from childhoods of a past when clothes were scarce and wearing a new dress for the first time was an event.)

When this photo is taken, my right breast and the submammary fold are a brownish color, burnt by cobalt, with blue crosses and red lines drawn on the skin to precisely indicate the area and the points to be irradiated. At the same time, I have been prescribed a postoperative chemotherapy protocol that is different from the previous one, and, every three weeks, for five days in a row, even at night, I have to wear a kind of harness, a belt around my waist with a fanny pack containing a plastic bottle, in the shape of a baby bottle, filled with chemotherapy products. It has a thin transparent plastic tube coming out of it, which threads up between my breasts to the collarbone, ending with a needle stuck into the catheter and covered by a dressing. Strips of adhesive tape hold the tube in place against the skin. Its heat causes the chemo liquids to rise and flow through my veins. Because of the bag on my belly, I cannot close my jacket or my coat, and I have difficulty hiding the plastic tubing attached to the bottle and threaded up under my sweater. When I am naked, with my leather belt, my vial of poison, my multicolored markings and the tube running across my upper body, I look like an extraterrestrial.

I no longer know what other photos were taken when I had this body. It didn't stop us from making love. He would say, "You're not a serious cancer patient."

If I think back to the prayer in the old missals, "Prayer to Ask of God the Proper Use of Sickness" by Blaise Pascal, it seems to me I have made the best possible use of cancer.

For months my body was a theater of violent operations.

During chemo sessions, with amusement I compared my body to a dishwasher, which inevitably came to mind, in view of the length of the program (between one hour and one and a half hours) and the introduction of a rinsing agent at the end. And my body never ceased to change: baldness and complete loss of body hair, scarring, and, in the weeks after the operation, in the hollow of my armpit, a sort of big orange filled with lymph that forced me to hold my arm away from my chest. Then the hair on my head grew back, fine and curly, my body hair like that of a prepubescent girl. My sense of smell became extremely acute. I detected all odors from a distance, even the ones that were usually the least noticeable. They were palpable. It was quite a discovery, and I liked sniffing the world like a dog. One day, at the hospice in Y., where I had gone to visit my last surviving aunt, I felt as though I could see the smell of food, of rancidness and urine, settled in a waxy layer on the faces of the men and women grouped around the TV, to the point of being able to touch the smell.

Nothing was frightening. I performed my task of cancer patient with diligence and viewed as an experience everything that happened to my body. (I wonder if doing as I do, not separating one's life from one's writing, does not mean spontaneously transforming experience into description.)

In the waiting room for radiotherapy at the Pontoise clinic, I kept seeing an issue of *Madame Figaro* whose cover featured a bare-breasted girl in a thin voile dress. Written in big letters were the words DARE TRANSPARENCY. In France, 11 percent of women have had, or currently suffer from breast cancer. More than three million women. Three million breasts stitched, scanned, marked with red-and-blue drawings, irradiated, reconstructed, hidden under blouses and T-shirts, invisible. Indeed we must dare to show them one day. (Writing about mine is part of this unveiling.)

I'd like to take you to Venice

There are the geometric elements of the tiles, the perspective, the morning light, the fact that the photo is vertical, and the essential, our clothes, contained almost entirely in the frame. It is impossible, looking at it, not to think back to the month when I took this photo, which coincides with my moving to rue du Faubourg Saint-Martin. The only decorative element in this partially furnished two-room apartment is a reproduction on the living room wall of *The Red Tower*, by Giorgio De Chirico. It represents a dungeon with a stretch of near-empty space at its foot, give or take a few details. I could, of course, have stored the picture in the cellar or another room, but the thought of facing this image, day after day, was quite appealing. When A. helped me to unpack my boxes, she told me that the original was in Venice. From then on, knowing we'd be going there the next month, I considered, pictured, the image as the projection of a desire that A. had expressed during our dinner of January 22, when we barely knew each other, and she had said: "I'd like to take you to Venice." Coming from her, and expressed so naturally, the sentence had touched me. At the time, I imagined that by dint of traveling together, it was inevitable that we would try to seduce each other on arrival. We were past that stage now. We shared a bed in Venice. First, in the cramped space of the Hotel Marconi—recommended by *Le guide du routard* for some reason that still escapes us—and then, probably thanks to a cancellation, in the calm of a pension in the Dorsoduro.

At the Peggy Guggenheim Collection, *The Red Tower* is exhibited in a room at the back of the ground floor. Same format as the reproduction in Paris. Not the same texture, however. That day, for reasons related to the talent A. applied to helping me discover and love her Venice (a far cry from the Rialto, San Marco, and Harry's Bar), for me an unbreakable bond was formed between this painting and our photos, which attempt to concentrate in a single space the unity of a moment essentially impossible to circumscribe.

Jeans sitting on the parquet

MAY 24 OR 31

when it's me taking the photo

In the living room, near the open door leading onto the hallway.

On the floorboards between a wall and the fringed edge of a rug, at the foot of a writing desk, a pair of jeans caves into itself, the legs stretched out in front. The black leather belt, unfastened but still woven through the belt loops, surrounds and supports an absent belly. Next to it, boxer shorts with red-and-white patterns and a puddle of black cloth. Impossible to say whether the piece of clothing belongs to M. or to me.

All we see of the wall is the chipped baseboard and a narrow strip of blue fabric pulled taut (the staples can be seen in the regular indentations at the very bottom), in which a square electrical outlet is embedded.

Near the seated jeans, we can also clearly see the two outstretched arms of a torso rising from the floor. There is something menacing about the life that emerges from clothes that have fallen in human postures. Monsters from the movie *Freaks*. The empty form of the body of M.

Of all the tales of war heard in my childhood, the most frightening was the one in which, after a bombing raid, all that remained of a man was his wheelchair next to a gas station.

The photo dates from three weeks after our trip to Venice, squeezed in with great difficulty between radiation therapy sessions. One afternoon, we took the elevator to the bell tower of San Giorgio Maggiore. The tourists already up there made their way down a few at a time, and we were alone. From where we stood, entwined, we could see the cloister just below, and the interior gardens of the convent of San Giorgio. I slipped off my bra under my T-shirt and threw it into the air, hoping it would fall into the cloister. It hovered for a long time, borne by the breeze in the opposite direction. It was one of the most graceful sights in the world. Then it drifted out of view. Afterward, in the elevator, we struggled to restrain our helpless laughter in front of its operator, a monk who rides up and down all day reading psalms. Once we were on the ground, M. searched for where the bra had landed. He found it in a deserted part of the quay and left it there.

It is always this image of the bra gently drifting in the air around San Giorgio that comes to mind when I think of that trip to Venice. Despite the scorching sun, we kept walking through the narrow streets and along the Zattere, in a sort of fluid state, blending into the dancing facades of the houses and the dazzling reflections of the sea. Orange-and-red banners hung from the windows, emblazoned with the word PACE, "peace," in big letters, protesting the war in Iraq. In the cemetery of San Michele, we amused ourselves by playing basketball with pebbles that we threw into trash cans. One evening, we pushed open the door of Harry's Bar, which until then I had never dared enter. All eyes turned to us with the look of jaded people hungry for new faces. We fled, bursting into laughter as soon as we were outside. In the hotel room, I photographed M. as a '70s rock star, shirtless with my wig and butterfly sunglasses.

Once I thought, "Cancer should become as romantic a disease as tuberculosis used to be."

Ever since we started writing about these photos, we have been in a state of photographic frenzy. We want to "take" each other, constantly—at the dinner table, or on waking in the morning. It's like an accelerating loss. The proliferation of photos, while intended to ward off the loss, only deepens it.

The click of the camera is a strange catalyst of desire that pushes you to go further. When it's me taking the photo, I feel a peculiar excitement in handling and adjusting the zoom, as if I had a male member—I think that many women experience this sensation. Each time the shutter is released, my brain quivers with pleasure. Anyone who does not also have an orgasm with the brain may not have experienced true pleasure. (*Before*, I would certainly have written all this in the imperfect tense, the purified tense of things that are finished, or which claim to be.)

Almost all the photos are taken in a single location, Cergy. Putting them all together, one could imagine that they were taken on the same day. They could be photos taken by a criminology squad, and our clothes could be all that's left of us, after our bodies have vanished for some unexplained reason.

We put ourselves in the shoes of the investigator. Did they leave their clothes behind? If so, why? Were they forced? Were they stripped before or after they were made to disappear? Who were the assailants? And what did they do with the bodies?

But in this image, only my clothes appear: black jeans, a shirt of the same color, pink boxers with little patterns on them. The trousers look as if they are sinking into the floor, unless they have just come out of the earth. Given the way they're arranged, and the shape, I certainly cannot have taken them off by myself. It makes me think of a rabbit skinned in a single motion, the way a glove is removed. I must have been barely ten when I first witnessed this display. It was in a suburban neighborhood in the north of France. At the beginning of the '70s, the Paris region still looked like the countryside, at least to me, who up until then had only lived in capital cities. Our neighbor had known my mother when she was a little kid. Now he was retired and spent most of his time tending his vegetable garden, his poultry yard and his hutches. I'd never seen a live rabbit, let alone a dead one. He showed me how he killed them with a sharp cuff to the back of the neck. Then he showed me how they were skinned and butchered. Anyway, we didn't eat rabbits at our place. We ate horsemeat almost every night. A topside or an oyster steak. We shopped at the only horsemeat butcher's in town, the Duvergers'. They were a stout couple with big, ruddy butchers' faces. I often went with my father to do errands, supposedly to give him a hand, but actually because I had a crush on Madame Duverger with her wide hips beneath her bloodstained work coat, her fleshy buttocks that I dreamed of touching, if only for ten seconds . . . Horsemeat eventually went out of fashion. Prices went up. My parents switched to pork and beef. The Duvergers, who had moved in behind the neighbor with the rabbits, started to look askance at us. The next year, they gave up their business, sold their bungalow and moved back to Brittany. Then one day the neighbor died. His wife kept the house, but the rabbits disappeared. She died soon after, and the house was sold by her children. It was the early 1980s, the beginning of the exodus. On the streets, FOR SALE signs multiplied. The old railway line was replaced by the RER, the shops near the station were bought up by insurance companies, temp agencies, and real estate offices.

Then it was my turn to sell. That was about the time this photo was taken. Like A. with her own mother's belongings, I kept a dress, a shirt, a scarf, and some stockings in a bag that I sometimes open, just—through the odor of burnt wood, mustiness, and lavender eau de cologne—for the sad pleasure of being abruptly plunged back into the time when she was there.

One day we went to Y. and stopped in front of the old café-grocery shop where A. had lived with her parents growing up. The house was for sale. A young man came out, mistaking us for buyers. A. was not keen on visiting, but we went in anyway. I discovered details that she had mentioned in her books, and I knew how she must be feeling. In a way, we could now feel that we were on an equal footing.

These trousers, from which the body has disappeared, are a little like that—rooms, an armchair, walls, a kitchen, an empty shell. To an outside eye, these are only traces. As for us, what we see are precisely the things that are not represented, those which happened before, during, and just after.

The white mules

EARLY JUNE

one or two songs

Again, morning light on this scene from the night, in the lounge part of the living room. To the left, in profile, the mass of the sofa covered in an orange damask fabric, to the right a small coffee table with gold, twisted legs on a blue carpet. In the background, the bottom of an open French window, the tiled floor of a balcony, the legs of a rattan table. On either side of the French window, the bottom shelves of the bookcase, barely visible, and a strip of midnight blue curtain. In this busy decor, a few items of clothing form fragile little heaps. Light summer things on the sofa, something that looks like a black shirt or T-shirt, a piece of brightly colored fabric sliding down the cushion, and on the carpet, a dress or skirt of the same fabric rolled up with a pair of beige trousers. Two white high-heeled mules walk toward the sofa. A little to the side are a pair of tan boat shoes, the left one resting on top of the right, like the shoes of adolescents in class when they're thinking about their papers, twisting their legs around each other. On the table, unreadable newspapers, an ashtray and a glass half-filled with white wine. The armrest cover has fallen off the sofa.

There's always a detail in the photo that grabs the eye, a detail more moving than others—a white label, a stocking snaking across the tiles, a lone sock rolled in a ball, a bra with its cups lying flat on the parquet, as if on display in a shop window. Here it's the white mules in front of the French window. It is already very hot, the summer to follow will be that of the "great heat wave" and when it's over thousands of old people will have died and been buried, even on Sundays, but for the time being, it was simply the most magnificent summer we had seen for a long time. The world under a white sky will shimmer all over, surreal, and morality will dissolve, as usual, in the heat.

We'll have dinner outside and I'll walk down the stairs to the garden, incredibly light in those white mules, with the music from the stereo turned up full blast, and this time I'll be thinking, "Another beautiful summer." Because for me all beauty, hope, and sadness are in that word "summer," and the titles of films in which it appears pierce my heart, *Summer with Monika*, *One Summer of Happiness*, *Summer of '42*. Summer, by dint of the word that designates it in the French language—été—is always experienced as already over. Summer can only *have been*. I was dazzled to be able to be so happy, to feel the same as at eighteen, when I had to live everything right away, as if I were going to stop being young once autumn arrived. In the garden, through the open windows, we heard Bryan Ferry, Elton John, Michel Polnareff, the Beatles.

The white mules are stopped in their tracks, and the music has died away.

Each season of our love affair is marked by a song or two that we never knew would be the one—the ones—to convey and indelibly condense the elusive succession of days.

IN THE WINTER THERE WAS:
William Sheller, "Un homme heureux"
Alain Souchon, "La vie ne vaut rien"
IN THE SPRING:
Elton John, "The One"
Fiona Apple, "I Know"
IN THE SUMMER:
Bryan Ferry, "These Foolish Things"
IN THE AUTUMN:
Art Mengo, "Je passerai la main" (but not for M.)
Elton John, "Tonight"
IN THE OTHER WINTER:
Mahalia Jackson, "In the Upper Room"
Christina Aguilera, "The Voice Within"

These songs will always be linked to M., as others are to other men for me, and to other women, for him. We should be wildly jealous of songs. It's enough to hear one by chance, in a shopping mall or a hair salon, to find myself transported not to a precise day but to a period of time whose changing skies and weather, diversity of world events, repetition of daily trajectories and actions—from eating breakfast to waiting on the Métro platform—have dissolved, as in a novel, into a single long day, cold or hot, dark or bright, colored by a single sensation, of happiness or unhappiness.

Photos cannot capture a span of time. They lock you into the moment. A song is expansion into the past, a photo is finitude. A song is the happy sensation of time, a photo its tragic side. I've often thought that one's whole life story could be told just with songs and photos.

(Will I remember a song associated with the writing of this text? No matter how I search, I can't think of a single one that could have played that mnemonic role. None that makes me say, "That was when I was writing *Cleaned Out*, or *Simple Passion*." For me, writing suspends all sensations other than those it brings to life and *shapes*.)

heat wave

It is morning. On the table, the remains of the previous night: an ashtray that is certainly full, a half-filled glass of white wine, my little rimmed glasses that I left there, probably when we started to take our clothes off. There, concentrated on the marble surface, are the first gestures of a myopic smoker who is about to make love, crushing out his cigarette, disposing of his glasses, though without them he will miss part of the *show*. Our footwear indicates that we have entered a different climatic universe: white mules for A., slip-ons for me. Not a sock in sight. In the background, near the window, are my light baggy cotton pants. In front of them, the skirt or top of the gauzy outfit A. often wears when the weather's hot. And it must be very hot. The heat wave has already begun, having arrived at the end of March. I realize that if I can date it with such precision, it is only thanks to the Salon du Livre, where I accompanied A. for a book signing. I can picture us on the same balcony that appears in the background. It was a Sunday, and the thought of having to get dressed and into the car, logging forty kilometers of asphalt along with a hefty dose of carbon dioxide, finding a place to park at Porte Maillot, and taking the Métro to Porte de Versailles, made us want only one thing—to enjoy the sunshine and the view over the Oise, and not go. We felt like school kids desperately looking for an excuse to get out of the history-geography test. As my memory is quite faithless, I depend on the rare obligations that A. agreed to, the trips taken because of invitations, to reconstruct the order of events in the photos.

As with each of the photos we selected, not by virtue of aesthetic criteria but because they seemed to us representative of a moment in our history, one detail predominates—and it is not the interplay of colors between the fabric of the sofa, the carpet, and the outfit A. wore that evening, nor even my shoes, whose tones match those of the coffee table (an old piano bench?), but this pair of mules, startlingly white. They seem to be following each other, walking one behind the other. It was an evening when we did not have dinner inside but in the garden. And though the mules seem to be heading for the sofa, I mainly see them coming down the stairs to the room I call "the crypt," which has cork-covered walls and for me is no more than an antechamber to our summer dinners on the lawn.

On either side of the French window, the edges of the living room bookshelves can be seen. From left to right, viewed in full, they hold French literature, foreign literature, sociology, all in alphabetical order. When I first saw this, I wondered how anyone could take the slightest pleasure in browsing through these books when their arrangement criteria are the same as those of a public library. At my place, and in my parents' house, books were arranged according to affinity or theme, with Thomas Mann within range of Proust, and Fitzgerald next to Hermann Hesse. Over time and frequent visits to Cergy, I got used to it. But with most of my books still in boxes, I don't know what my "ideal literary space" will end up looking like.

Bedroom

END OF MAY–BEGINNING OF JUNE

the invisible scene

It is a very spare photo, almost entirely filled by a pale green carpet on which the vacuum cleaner has left trails going in all directions. The light from an invisible window forms a white gully. At the back of this milky green sea, in the open doorway, is a dark cluster with two pale splotches in the center and two men's loafers with a gap in between. One sits on top of something blue. In the foreground on the left, a large section of white damask bedspread spills down in folds, like a curtain. At the bottom of the bedspread are two tangled scarves, one multicolored, the other two-toned. A third scarf, beige and wound around itself, falls limply from the bed like a piece of rope.

No two clothing compositions are alike. Each is a unique construction—there's no doubt about it—whose laws and causes escape us. Perhaps nature is what remains of the desire of a vanished god, of his immense orgasm, the big bang in which he disintegrated, and at the origin of the world, there is the same principle that endlessly throws living beings against each other.

There is nothing of our bodies in the photos. Nothing of the love we made. The invisible scene. The pain of the invisible scene. The pain of the photograph. It comes from wanting something other than what is. The *boundless* meaning of the photograph. A hole through which the fixed light of time, of nothingness is perceived. Every photo is metaphysical.

It is said in the Gospel according to John that Mary Magdalene, when she came to see Christ after his death, found the tomb empty. All that remained were the cloths in which the body had been wrapped, lying on the ground, and the shroud which had been placed over the head of Jesus *non cum linteaminibus positum, sed separatim involutum in unum locum*, "not put with the cloths but folded separately and put in another place."

A few months ago, in the winter, we went to the Montparnasse Cemetery to visit the grave of M.'s grandparents. All the gravestones were covered with snow and M. was not sure that the grave we had stopped in front of was the right one. He tried to sweep away the snow with his hands to see the name, but the snow was frozen. I looked among our things for an object we could use to clear the ice with. The most effective solution would have been to urinate on it, but that was a hard thing to accept doing. In the end,

M. used the sharp edge of his key ring. The first and last names of his grandfather appeared, Louis Marie, then those of his grandmother, Mathilde Marie. I imagined my name on the stone instead. I saw it very clearly, but it wasn't real.

When I look at our photos, it is my body's disappearance that I see. However, what matters to me is not that my hands or face have ceased to exist, or that I can no longer walk, eat, or fuck. It's the disappearance of thought. Several times I've said to myself that if my thoughts could continue elsewhere, dying wouldn't matter to me.

Last year M. said: "You always wanted to write as if you were going to die afterward, well, here you are, my darling!" He was referring to something I'd written two years earlier in a book. There I was, indeed, but it didn't change anything, and when I was writing I forgot that I could die. It's an illusion to believe that truth only comes to the fore when you die. So my position was false.

How to conceive of my death? The physical form of a corpse, its icy cold and silence, and later its decomposition, doesn't matter to me—there's no point in thinking about it, and there's nothing to doubt about it—that's the way things go. That, I've seen. I mean thinking about my nonexistence. Inexorably I am a body inside of time. I cannot conceive of my exit from time. None of what awaits us is thinkable. But that's just the point: there'll be no more waiting. Or memory. (There was that ad in the Métro two years ago: "We rarely remember our old age.")

I now realize that the only thing that can justify scientific and philosophical endeavor, and art, is not knowing what nothingness is. And if the shadow of nothingness, in one form or another, does not hover over writing, even of a kind most acquiescent to the beauty of the world, it doesn't really contain anything of use to the living. That shadow is in *Phaedra*, Book VI of the *Confessions*, *Madame Bovary*, *In Search of Lost Time*, *Nausea*, the music of Bach, Mozart, the paintings of Watteau and Schiele.

Here, the unity of color—white bedspread, white wall, pale green carpet—transforms the room into a disembodied space, where I no longer see any sign of our having been there, but only our absence, even our death. The multicolored clutch of scarves is a crawling monster that has made its nest under the bed. Concentrated in the doorway, our clothes seem to have been snatched up by an invisible hand.

On May 24, A.'s last chemo bag is removed. A chapter is closing, and with it, the time when we took the first photos, all inseparable from the time that preceded them.

Four months earlier, I accompanied A. for the first time to the Institut Curie, where her tumor was going to be removed. We had a drink at the Carrefour de l'Odéon just before, as if it were a day like any other. Even though I am aware that she has to undergo surgery under general anesthetic, and that her life—therefore our relationship—depends on the success of the operation, as we walk side by side down the rue d'Ulm, holding hands, the tone is playful and lighthearted. The tragic tendency, to which the socialized individual seems to be subject, is replaced by a childlike joy at having met each other. Without having planned it, we are laying the foundations for a parenthetical temporality, a journey with no end in view. At the gates of the Institut, I tell myself that I will leave A. at the reception and go home because I have no business being there. But our footsteps do not break pace with each other. A. fills in the admission forms, is told which floor to go to, and I follow all the way to her room that looks out on the rooftops.

I don't remember anything after that, only that I stayed with her until nightfall. My presence in that place, like hers, seemed to be a matter of course. The next day, she had the operation. Day after day, I take the RER, get off at Luxembourg station, and walk the rest of the way. The streets, the shops, and the restaurants where the local workers gather at lunchtime grow familiar. I always look in amazement at the grocer's with my family name on the sign, at the corner of rue Saint-Jacques and rue Gay-Lussac. I always warn her of my arrival. When I enter the room, she always has her wig on, although in the first nights I spent in Cergy, I had many opportunities to feel the smooth touch of her scalp against my cheek when her "Simone de Beauvoir" turban slipped off. We talk, we laugh a lot, and discuss the Matzneff book I've given her. On Saturday, snow covers the roofs. We look at it together, but I don't ask myself what she is feeling. We are *in the moment.*

Is it possible to feel nostalgic about a moment entirely conditioned by the possibility of death? That is what this photo says to me. It marks a journey back to the happy days at the Institut Curie.

Brussels, Hôtel Les Écrins, Room 125

OCTOBER 6

But she's ugly!

On a black background, a strange green object with a rounded shape, a dark border, dark spots and a foot, radiating a yellow light. It looks like a poisonous mushroom that, due to a kind of short, thick growth extending from its cap, seems to be wearing a severed penis. Or like a Martian whose head appears to be adorned with an indefinable organ that may act as an antenna, perched on a device that lights up the night.

In reality, it's a very ordinary bedside lamp whose bulb is covered with a toothbrush glass, itself draped in a wash mitt that is slipping down on one side. I can't tell whether it's the glass or the wash mitt that gives it a green color. In this harshly lit room, this was the only way we could find to create a softer, indeed, a more funereal light.

This is the first photo taken after lovemaking since the end of June. There are no photos of the time between July and October. M. was often away, in Karlsruhe, in Montpellier, in Mauritania. I suspected him of having another woman. But maybe the only reason for the lack of photos was that we had very few clothes to remove, due to the scorching heat.

My cancer treatment had ended two months earlier, and my hair had grown back five centimeters. It rained almost nonstop and there was an icy wind for the three days spent in Brussels. We went back to café Poechenellekelder, near the Manneken Pis fountain, where the two customers who sit drinking on a bench at the bar remain motionless for so long that people start to wonder before realizing they are dummies with wax faces.

In a shop selling old records, I recognized the cover of an Édith Piaf 45 that I'd bought when I was sixteen because of the song "Les amants d'un jour." It had a blue cover. I'd later given away or resold this 45, as I'd begun to turn my nose up at anything that wasn't "quality music." There, in that shop in Brussels, I wanted to have it, not for "Les amants d'un jour"—which I'd heard too many times, its emotion exhausted for me—but for the blue cover, and for another song on the record that I'd completely forgotten, "Soudain une vallée." M. bought it for me.

On October 7, he asserted: "I've never been with a woman as feminist as you. Not by a long shot." I didn't ask him to say more. Suddenly, it was as if we didn't know each other. I don't really know what it's like not to be a feminist, or how women behave toward men who don't see them as feminists. That same month, when I opened a book belonging to M.,

I came across a photo of a young woman with a child and an older woman. It took me a while to realize that the young woman was his previous partner. When he told me about her at the start of our relationship, M. had said, “She’s got a nice body, but her face is not so great.” My first reaction to the photo was triumph, as I looked at her nose and chin, saying, “But she’s ugly!”—and then anger at myself for having created a perfect image of her which made me feel inferior. Then I was overcome with sadness. It was worse for me that M. had loved this woman with her graceless features. His love for her only seemed more intense. I would have preferred her to be beautiful so I could explain his attachment to her on aesthetic grounds, both banal and objective.

I don’t know how to use the language of feelings while “believing” it. When I try, it seems fake to me. I only know the language of things, of material traces, visible evidence. (Although I never stop trying to transmute it into words and ideas.) I wonder if contemplating and describing our photos is not a way of proving to myself that his love exists, and in the face of the evidence, the material proof they embody, of dodging the question for which I see no answer, “Does he love me?”

The wallpaper was atrocious. The room overlooked zinc roofs. To soften the harsh lighting, we put a toothbrush glass covered with a wash mitt over the wall lamp. I was afraid that it would catch fire and us with it.

One afternoon, we returned to rue du Midi, where we'd barely set foot during our visit in March. In this working-class district that connects the Bourse to place Rouppe, which in the '80s abounded in shops selling comic book albums, there remained only two or three still devoted to comics. I wanted to take A. to the crêperie where I'd once been a regular, but it too had disappeared, replaced by a trendy bar. As for the squalid buildings adjoining the terminal for buses to Uccle, they had been partially restored: facadism, an old Brussels craze. But that didn't bother me. Coming to Brussels with A. also meant recreating my adopted city, and giving my childhood a chance to fade away.

Between July and October, there's a void. Of the few photos we took that summer, there were none of our clothes on the floor. What we couldn't see again had not taken place. Also, I had completely stopped writing my diary in the spring. We'd left no trace in other words.

The only images that come to mind are those of evenings spent in Cergy and the stifling heat that shrouded the days in a halo of unreality. In the afternoon, A. bought a solid piece of beef, or a nice sea bream. As soon as the lawn below the house was completely engulfed in shadow, I would start to prepare the barbecue. There was a cast-iron garden table painted white and four matching chairs. The windows of the crypt were left wide open so we could hear the music playing from inside. Every time I came over, I burned a CD beforehand, made up of tracks I'd downloaded from the Net. Jazz standards, French chanson, pop. Of the dozens of titles we listened to on those nights, only a few seem to me to reveal the essence of those hot, full hours, spent at a total remove from the affairs of the world, of that heat-wave summer. The impression is misleading insofar as songs recorded in the spring mingle in the same space-time in my mind with songs recorded the following winter. My only certainty lies in the emblematic and personal character that a song may have had for us as compared to another. In historical order, as much as in our order of preference, our Top Nine is as follows: "Un homme heureux" (William Sheller), "These Foolish Things" (Bryan Ferry), "She's Leaving Home" (The Beatles), "La mer n'existe pas" (Art Mengo), "Bruxelles" (Dick Annegarn), "The One" (Elton John), "I Know" (Fiona Apple), "Tonight" (Elton John again), "The Voice Within" (Christina Aguilera). These songs are so deeply rooted in our relationship that I've damned myself, in making them our companions, to never being able to listen to them again without them taking me back to Cergy, from here to eternity. Tunes that I know every bar of, most of which seemed to me to be wonderfully suited to the place and the atmosphere—the candlesticks, the Premières Côtes de Blaye, the invisible presence of the river Oise below us in the valley. The bell tower of Cergy's old church, illuminated every evening, the volume of the stereo turned up full blast on soccer match nights to drown out the sound of the TV that the neighbors had set up on their porch.

I found the image of myself on those evenings very funny, standing statue-like before the barbecue, a meat fork in one hand and a hair dryer in the other. After all, I was no better or worse than the people wielding the same tools two hundred meters or ten kilometers away. Nonetheless, behind the symbolic value of my domestic arsenal was the reality of where I was. Before I started using it, the barbecue in question stood tucked away against a wall, as if it had been retired. The cooking tool, a little rusty, looked as if it hadn't been used for a long time. Nearby, a pile of extremely dry logs seemed to be waiting for an improbable fire to be built in the hearth with its unusable chimney, where bees had made their home for many years.

When we started having our dinner on the lawn, I didn't feel that I was simply using the premises, but giving it a second birth, as if, since her divorce, A. had walled up this recreational and familial part of her life. I'm probably wrong in thinking this.

Bedroom

CHRISTMAS MORNING

the first time with a man

Photo taken at floor level. On the right is the three-quarter size bed, whose white-painted bedposts and spindled headboard are half-drowned in shadow, as is the carpet. The rumpled white duvet forms a mountain in the middle of the bed and cascades into a heap at the foot. On the carpet that is bleached by the light a black pump with straps and a very high heel, poking halfway out from under the bed, stands upright like a sort of limited-edition item in a display case. The other pump is under the bed, upside down, in the shadows. In the background, the French window opens onto a balcony railing, with the sky behind. The carpet and the sky are the same pale color so the room seems to be floating in the sky. A kind of peace emanates from the scene, similar to that of catalog ads for bed linen. Between the bed and the French window, almost indistinguishable, are the white hind legs of the cat Kyo. There is nothing belonging to M. in this photo.

Another room with the same kind of sweetness overlaps this one, the room from last winter at the Institut Curie, on the third floor. I remember today that in that room I remembered the one I was in at the Hôtel-Dieu in Rouen just after my abortion, when I was twenty-three. Do we not see life behind us as a series of rooms within rooms within rooms, all the way back to the one that is forever opaque, and snowy like a poorly recorded videotape, the room of birth?

For years, my husband and I searched for the ideal bed. It had to look like Brigitte Bardot's, which we had seen in *Marie Claire,* monumental, Napoleon III–style. In the meantime, we just slept on a box spring and mattress on four legs, one of which had been broken and was replaced by an upside-down saucepan with a book on top: a pocket edition of Claudel's (very long) play *The Satin Slipper.* Each time I noticed it, I thought of Sacha Guitry's remark "Lucky he doesn't have the pair." Finally we found our bed in the catalog of a little shop on the rue du Faubourg Saint-Antoine, a bed with columns and a headboard made of sculpted bars that almost touched the ceiling. It was a model made in Spain and had to be ordered. We waited six months. By the time it arrived, we hadn't made love for five months and we broke up three years later. I kept the bed. It's the one in the photo.

When, as an adolescent, I imagined making love, it was in a forest, a wheat field, or by the sea. I didn't think it was possible to lie in a bed, as parents do, with a man not your husband. Only whores and "women of ill repute" did that. At the age of seventeen, I found myself in a bed with a boy for an entire night. There is an expression that perfectly captures the power and the shock of the event, *ne pas en revenir*—to never come back from it. In the exact sense of the expression, I never did come back, I never rose from that bed.

The strangeness of sleeping with a man for the first time. I undoubtedly belong to the first generation of women more familiar with the continually renewed astonishment of random beds than with the habit of the marriage bed.

For a long time, people did not show their beds readily. For a woman not to make her bed during the day was considered by her neighbors to be the ultimate proof that she was letting things slide, the surefire sign of her inability to run a household. It made her look undeserving in the eyes of all to expose the open, rumpled sheets, complete with stains and the imprint of bodies, without shame. If you weren't going to give your sheets and blankets a good shake out the window, at least you had to COVER your bed.

It was in unmade beds that I learned to read stains. All women are readers of stains, heir to the obligation to wash, to clean, and, "*according to the nature of the stain*," as the advice in the magazines says, to "get it out."

We continue to take photos. It is an activity that can go on indefinitely since no two scenes are ever the same. Its only limits are those of desire. But it seems to me that we no longer view the spectacle we discover in the way we did before.

We no longer feel the pain that drove us to make a record of the scene in the first place. Taking the photo is no longer the last thing we do. It's part of our writing process. A form of innocence has been lost.

Who would have thought from looking at this photo that it was Christmas morning?

One year earlier, just a few days before we met, I'd sent A. an email in which I told her how little I liked the holiday season. It wasn't Christmas per se that bothered me, but the commercial circus surrounding it, the buying frenzy that came over people as of mid-November. From the tone of her reply, it was clear that we both felt the same. For my part, I was preparing to celebrate Christmas with the family of my future ex: her daughter, her father, her maternal grandmother, and her aunt, a Catholic nun. A distressing memory, for I felt so out of place, pretending to be in good spirits while our relationship was falling apart.

I have no memories of happy Christmases. Not since I was a child. My grandparents, who lived in Paris, made the trip to Brussels each year. They would stay for a few days. I used to look at them in disbelief, the way you'd look in a shop window with a real family on display. I dreaded the moment when they'd have to leave again. Many years later, for the fifteen Christmases that followed my father's death, I tried to put a smile back on my mother's face, if only for one evening. Neither she nor I was fooled by this charade. But we played along. Because there was nothing else to do.

The French window lets in bright light. The cold cannot be perceived anywhere. Behind the foot of the bed, you can make out Kyo's paws. She had slipped in there, and I had seen her through the viewfinder but wanted to include her in one of these moments from which she was usually excluded. My clothes are nowhere to be seen. They are probably on the chair that permanently remains at the far left side of the room. Alone under the bed are A.'s high heels. It's as if I weren't there, as if I were absent from the world as I was for all those joyless Christmases. Meanwhile on the floor below, a decorated fir tree stands on display in the living room with our two pairs of shoes beneath it.

Bedroom

CHRISTMAS MORNING, continued

it's not my body

Against the pale green background of the carpet, a purple, pink, and black bra, black stockings with a wide lace border, and a suspender belt are tangled together in a disturbing jumble that forms a floral composition. The bra, with one of its cups turned inside out, sits on top like a large pair of glasses. A filigree of suspenders and straps in the shape of a figure eight slips out of the jumble. Beside it, M.'s black T-shirt with white stripes spreads and creases to form another dark flower with a little white arrow—the label—in the middle. There are no other objects, apart from a strip of orange cushion. Nothing but the increasingly commercial and commonplace props of private erotic theater, the customary garb that I hate to wear in the car for fear of a serious accident that would expose me to all and sundry in my thong and stockings, and which I never wear to write in, as if it would prevent me from doing so. These undergarments always feel like a disguise, probably because when I was fourteen, on getting home from the cinema where *The Foreign Legion* was playing, with whores in corsets and black stockings, I dressed up as one of them, after a fashion, in my swimsuit and scraps of fabric, and imagined myself pulling back the beaded curtain in a soldiers' bar and closing it behind the man who had just entered.

I don't feel anything when I look at this photo. Really, what I see is not me or my body, whose remains this floral composition is, but the mannequin who wore the Lise Charmel thong, bra, and suspender belt—pink and purple flowers on a black background—in the window of the Orcanta boutique at Trois Fontaines, last winter.

The summer sales have begun. The boutiques in the shopping center are bursting with clothes. This afternoon, I went down to the basement of Mango. Women and very young girls were raking through piles of T-shirts in the bins, compulsively flipping through the rows of dresses on the racks, unhooking hangers and rushing to queue up for the dressing rooms to the rhythm of deafening rap (so this music originally intended for revolt is now used to plunge shoppers into a state of hypnosis?). I had the sensation of being trapped in a female pandemonium. I abhorred this blind rushing about, the state of greed I'd fallen prey to before, in which nothing in the world was more important than possessing a top at 30 percent off. I hurried out again, passing the only man I saw in the shop, the black security guard pacing up and down by the entrance. I asked myself if sales were not the enchanted form of people's debasement by capitalism, the desecration of things and of the labor—so poorly paid—which goes into producing them. I thought tenderly of the compositions formed by our clothes abandoned after lovemaking, so far removed from these anonymous heaps. Photographing them seemed to me a way of restoring dignity to these things that we keep so close—an attempt, in a way, to make them our *sacred ornaments*.

In Rome, in a street near the Largo di Torre Argentina, there is a luxury clothing shop for ecclesiastics, De Ritis. The shop window on the left is devoted to men's vestments: albs, splendidly embroidered, and sumptuous chasubles in pink, silver, and gold. In the window on the right, for women, are civilian clothes only, skirts, blouses, shapeless cardigans in brown, gray, midnight blue, in the style of the 1950s in the provinces. The Church, faithful to the theory of the natural order, reserves seduction and beauty for men: the plumage of males is resplendent, that of females drab. On New Year's Eve, M. and I observed a nun who stood transfixed in front of the women's window. After several minutes of contemplation, she entered purposefully, as if moved by an irrepressible desire. We watched her from outside. At the counter she was presented with a gray cardigan.

Photos lie, always.

I have often been struck by holiday photos, where couples stand side by side with radiant offspring at the height of summer bliss. You think you'd like to be in their shoes. You forget that ten days later, the couple separated. That for the next six months they fought over custody of the kid. That the photos will be taken from their Ikea frames and end up at the bottom of a box.

The previous shot, for me the epitome of solitude, is belied by this one, taken in the same room at the same time. A.'s lingerie lies next to my boxers at the foot of a large orange cushion. Here is the rawest incarnation of our physical love—underwear falling to the floor, the ultimate foreplay. As well as the forgetting of my adolescence.

At fifteen I wore polyester trousers that made my legs itch. Leaning on the balustrade of the Youth and Culture Center, I watched my little friends stand around waiting for the gate of the Collège Saint-Exupéry to open. I remained on the sidelines. They stood in little clusters, boys on one side, girls on the other, almost all of them wearing Levi's 501s and khaki shirts unearthed from American surplus shops in the region. I wanted to be one of them, but I didn't know how to go about it. With my nylon shirts and the good grades on my school essays, I was excluded from the start, condemned to all manner of bullying. My dream was to have a pair of jeans and choose them myself. I didn't even know what it felt like to wear jeans, how a person felt inside them. Fitting into the group meant wearing a uniform: theirs.

As much as I hated the way my father clothed me, I also found my body *unsightly* when I undressed at night. Still I looked, with my back to the mirror and craning my neck to try to see what my buttocks were like.

Looking at myself horrified me. All I could see was my lack of muscle and body hair, my protuberant ribs, my pelvis that was far too wide for a boy's. And yet each night I started all over. Reduced to existing solely in my reflection in the mirror, the fact of being naked, stripped of the trappings of the schoolboy Marc Marie, forged from a model designed by his parents, was somehow comforting. No matter how ugly I found it, this body invisible to others was mine.

The same goes for these photos. They don't show me, but I'm looking straight into the mirror.

The rose rock

JANUARY 7, 2004

the paradox of photography

A black beast with a huge head and an atrophied body ending in a heart-shaped appendage seems to be tumbling down a yellow wall, along with an object bent into a V shape, a boot twisted into a V, and a large desert rose, made of stone. Underneath is another boot, folded over on itself, which has landed on a pale floor. There is no perspective in this tableau, in which the yellow wall and white floor are extensions of each other. Everything appears flat, weightless, immaterial, caught in a long slow descent, like Don Juan as played by Michel Piccoli in the Marcel Bluwal film, whirling toward hell to the music of Mozart's Requiem.

It is as if M. has photographed an abstract canvas in a picture gallery. It is impossible for me to spontaneously see in this yellow wall the green bedroom carpet, which the morning sun, as it moved, made paler and divided into two zones of color where our underwear and my boots are strewn. Impossible to see in the rose made of stone the dress I wore just that one time—it's too short, and trimmed with multiple ribbons that had to be threaded through loops, making me wonder what kind of contortions I must have performed to get it off. Everything is transfigured and disembodied. That is the paradox of this photo, intended to give our love more reality but which instead makes it unreal. Before this photo, I feel nothing. Here there is no more life or time. Here I am dead.

This photo could be named after A.'s dress, the desert rose. Because of its color and its dessicated look. It is an out-of-season dress. Very short. Too short. I'm not sure A. wore it any other night.

I had to climb up on the bed to take the photo. At the time, it was very beautiful. Too beautiful. In the end, this image embodies the limitations of our work: photos in which aesthetics dominate are short on meaning.

Each of the first photos was born of a detail. I focused on a specific point, and tried as much as possible to avoid using the flash by inflating the camera sensitivity and "pushing" the film. Then my field of vision widened. It was no longer simply the contrast between two pieces of clothing that I was trying to capture, or the reflection of natural light on the leather of a shoe, but the scene as a whole. I was trying to encompass all the different dramaturgic layers of the play that we had just performed for ourselves alone.

For several months, A. refused all invitations. Chemo and radiotherapy made any travel to another country impossible. As soon as we were able, we left. We made several trips in a very short period. We had to make up for lost time, to enjoy every moment to the full. But as soon as it was time to return to France, I became aware of the fleeting quality of all we had experienced. I'd find myself back in my little apartment on the fifth floor, despairing at my inability to hold onto happiness.

One day when I had just arrived back from a trip, a grayer day than others, I pulled the photos out. Not the ones from trips, but these ones. And my sadness was allayed.

Lined up next to each other, these snapshots are like a diary to me. A diary of 2003. Love and death. The decision to exhibit them, make a book of them, is to put the seal on a part of our history.

I don't know what these photos are. I know what they embody, but I don't know what they're for.

I know what they are not: images in frames on a mantelpiece, next to a father, chubby babies, and a great-uncle in uniform.

At what point did I stop thinking and saying, "I have cancer," and start to say, "I had cancer"? I feel as though I am still between the two, in a zone of uncertainty because at any time I could slide back from the second state into the first, my cancer having *recurred*. But if I measure the reality of my cancer in terms of last year's indifference to things that interest the majority of people—my remoteness from world events of that time—and the unreality of cancer in terms of the anger they provoke in me again, the quite futile preoccupations I engage in anew, and the stretch of future that I have granted myself by taking out a five-year guarantee on a dishwasher, for example, then I can say, "I *had* cancer."

For months, my body was investigated and photographed innumerable times from every angle and with every technique in existence.[4] I realize now that I neither saw nor wanted to see anything of the *inside* of my skeleton and organs. I had to wonder each time I was examined *what more* they would find.

The catheter was removed last April. I wore it inside me for a year and a half. Over time it became like a kind of jewel inlaid in my skin near the shoulder. I asked the doctor to give it to me and said I wanted to keep it. It was the first time he had received such a request, and he laughed: "To remember this by?" I also kept the wig. I saw it recently at the back of a drawer and I thought, "I may never again have the chance to feel such strong emotion," and at the same time I thought, "I'm mortal and I'm alive."

I can no longer abide novels or films with fictional characters suffering from cancer. What possesses those authors, how do they dare to *invent* these kinds of stories? Everything about them seems fake, to the point of being ridiculous.

I've spread out all the photos on the table in the living room. They look like the cards from a game of Clue, where all you can see of the house and the different rooms are the floors, the baseboards of the partitions, the bottoms of doors, the legs of furniture. No murder weapon, just the repeated signs of a struggle. Without thinking, I took a photo of the whole thing. Perhaps to give myself the illusion of capturing a whole. All of our story. But it's not there. In a few years, these photos

4 Mammogram; drill biopsy of the breast; ultrasound of the breasts, liver, gallbladder, bladder, uterus, heart; lung X-ray; cardiac amyloidosis scan; MRI of the breasts and bones; scanner of the breasts, abdomen, and lungs; a positron emission tomography, or PET scan. I am probably forgetting a few.

may hold no interest for either of us, except as testimonials to shoe fashion in the early 2000s.

Soon we will exchange our texts. I'm afraid of seeing what he's written. I'm afraid of seeing his otherness, a dissimilarity of points of view concealed by desire and the sharing of daily life, which writing will unveil in one fell swoop. Does writing separate or unite? I would like for him not to have written because of me, or for me, but outside of me, looking outward at the world. As for me, when I was writing I didn't think of him reading what I'd done, I don't know what I wrote *in relation to* him. I wonder if I haven't simply explored and brought together in a text the twofold fascination I've always had with photography and the material traces of presence. A fascination, now more than ever, with time.

I can see us again on a Sunday in February, a fortnight after my operation, in Trouville. We stayed on the bed all afternoon. It was bitterly cold and bright. The purple night fell. I was crouched over M., his head between my thighs, as if he had just come out of my belly. It occurred to me at the time that there should have been a photo. With the title *Birth.*

Works by
ANNIE ERNAUX

In order of publication in English, followed by the dates of original publication in French.

Cleaned Out
1974

A Woman's Story
1988

A Man's Place
1983

Simple Passion
1992

A Frozen Woman
1981

Exteriors
1993

Shame
1997

"I Remain in Darkness"
1997

Happening
2000

The Possession
2002

Things Seen
2000

The Years
2008

A Girl's Story
2016

Do What They Say or Else
1977

Getting Lost
2001

Look at the Lights, My Love
2014

The Young Man
2022

I Will Write to Avenge My People:
The Nobel Lecture
2023

The Use of Photography with Marc Marie
2005

Writing, the Other Life
2022

L'autre Fille
2011

L'atelier noir
2011

Une Conversation with Rose-Marie Lagrave
2023